WULF

ff

WULF

Kevin Crossley-Holland

illustrated by Gareth Floyd

faber and faber

LONDON · BOSTON

First published in 1988
by Faber and Faber Limited
3 Queen Square London WC1N 3AU

Printed in Great Britain by
Richard Clay Ltd Bungay Suffolk

British Library Cataloguing in Publication Data

Crossley-Holland, Kevin
Wulf.
I. Title   II. Floyd, Gareth
823'.914[J]

ISBN 0-571-15100-0

for Kieran and Dominic
as it was in the beginning

Contents

Note

Cedd (pronounced 'Ched') began his missionary work among the East Saxons in AD 653. In 656 King Æthelwald granted him land to build a monastery at Ythancestir (pronounced 'Oothanchester') which is the present-day Bradwell-on-Sea in Essex. Cedd constructed his church on the site of the Roman shore fort of Othona, using the Roman building materials, and brought monks to the monastery south from his native Northumbria. And this church, St Peter-on-the-Wall, one of the oldest churches in England, still stands for all to see, a great isolated fist up against saltmarshes and the sea.

King Æthelwald was Æthelhere's younger brother. In the first episode I have referred to Æthelhere's death in the battle of the River Winwæd (pronounced 'Weenwad') on 15 November 655. His body was lost in the river, which was in flood.

The action of the second episode takes place in the summer of 657, a little more than a year after the building of the church and the monastery. The monks' daily celebration of the Divine Office, referred to in this episode, consisted of seven services: Matins, Prime, Tierce, Sext, Nones, Vespers and Compline. The midnight service was Nocturns.

It was in 654 that Cedd founded a monastery at Lastingham in the North Yorkshire Moors. In *A History of the English Church and People*, the Venerable Bede (*c.* 673–735) wrote: 'Cedd chose a site for the monastery among some high and remote hills, which seemed more suitable for the dens of robbers than for human habitation. His purpose in this was to fulfil the prophecy of Isaiah: "In the habitation of dragons, where each lay, shall be grass with reeds and rushes."' Nothing tangible remains today of Cedd's northern foundation, although the present church, with its magnificent crypt (begun in 1078) probably incorporates stones from the older monastery.

The idea of describing Cedd's relationship with Wulf first suggested itself when I read Bede's reference to the single boy survivor among those monks who went north to Lastingham, and I should mention that I have made so bold as to advance the date of Cedd's death by five years. But Bede has very little to say about Cedd's personality (and nothing about Wulf), so both their characters and the course of their friendship are entirely fictional.

The Sea-Stranger

'Wulf!' bellowed the woman. 'Wulf! Wulf!' Her voice sounded like some great horn.

Wulf pretended not to hear. He sat against the outside of their hut, scraping, scraping at a piece of bone with his stubby knife. He had been working at it all day, whittling the bone to a long thin strip. Whenever he paused, his right arm ached, and the ache made him more determined than ever to cut some of the teeth in the bone before nightfall. As he worked he muttered:

> *What am I? I have white teeth*
> *that cannot bite. I scrape about*
> *carved from bone . . .*

'Wulf! Wulf! where are you?' blasted his mother, for all the world like the trumpeting north wind itself.

And then his sister Anna came trotting out of the hut, screwing up her eyes against the September sunlight, calling 'Woof, Woof . . .'

Wulf sighed. He carefully put his knife and the half-carved bone into the pocket in his tunic, and stood up.

'Woof!' said Anna.

'I'm coming,' said Wulf. He walked round the little timber hut to the doorway. It was so gloomy inside that at first he could see nothing. And as for his mother, her eyes were so swollen that she could barely see Wulf. She heard him, though, and at once raised herself from her bed of bristling straw.

'Where have you been?' she boomed. And then, without waiting for a reply, 'You're not like your brother. Oswald has worked like a man. For two years he's worked in the fields.'

'What was he like?' said Wulf.

'Who?'

'My father. I can't really remember.'

'I'm talking about you, not your father,' said Wulf's mother. 'You sit around, dreaming and singing, carving bits of wood and bone all day.'

4

'How are your eyes?' said Wulf.

'Terrible,' said his mother. And terrible they were: inflamed and oozing. 'It's surely because of this scolding wind,' she said. 'Nothing good ever came out of the north. Go and get me a crab.'

'Cwab,' said Anna.

'A crab?' said Wulf, surprised. 'Why?'

'Questions, you're always asking questions,' said his mother.

'I just want . . .'

'To know,' said his mother. 'Well, don't you know that a crab is the only cure for swollen eyes?'

'Nobody told me that,' said Wulf.

'Get me a live crab,' said his mother. 'Pull out its eyes and put them on the back of my neck. That way, the swelling will go.'

Wulf stepped out of the hut. He ran past the other huts in the hamlet of Ythancestir and past Earl Athulf's hall, then took the sandy path that led straight to the old disused stone fort and, just beyond it, the rough-tongued sea. Gasping for breath, Wulf tore through the great undefended gateway and threw himself on to the fort's grass floor. He closed his eyes; his breathing lengthened.

What happens, Wulf wondered, if people just go on running? Do they burst like a pig's bladder? Or do they get so tired that they can't go any further? He thought about it for a while and then, still undecided, opened one eye, stood up and began to patrol round the inside of the fort's great

5

walls. Parts of the four walls had collapsed into great mounds of stone; parts looked as if they might fall if Wulf so much as leaned against them; but other parts still stood firm, towering over him. He picked at the lichen and marvelled at the way in which the stone blocks had been cut, and laid in rows one on top of another, bonded by some strange stony mortar. 'My place,' Wulf said to himself. 'Made by giants.'

And it was true, Wulf was just about the only person ever to come to the old fort except for Anna; and Anna, thought Wulf, she is only two anyway. He shared the place with the screaming birds and the soft, growing grass. He shared with it his secrets – especially his secret memories about his father who had been killed in battle and buried far off in Mercia. A laughing man . . . strong . . . grey eyes . . .

Sometimes Wulf asked the old men in the hamlet who had built the fort, and why. He always got the same answers. 'The giants – the Romans – made it' and 'It was made before any of us can remember.' And again, 'We build in wood, not stone. It was made even before we came to this country.' So Wulf had to be satisfied with these half-answers; he thought grown-ups usually gave half-answers anyway. 'My place,' he said again, feeling the reliable stone, more at home and happy than anywhere else in the world.

A dark cloud scuttled across the sky and obscured the sun, and the sudden change in the

6

light and pincer-nip in the air was enough to change Wulf's mood too. He hurried across the fort, hoping to find a crab in the shallow water chopping and slopping against the outside of the massive north-eastern wall. Wulf had once measured that wall; it was more than three times as thick as he was long.

For three days the wind had been nagging at the sea. Wulf stood in the water gateway, at the top of the slimy landing steps, and looked out at the fluid black shield, the silver spears shattering. He heard the water roar as the flint-grey rollers raced to the shore, and the sight and sound filled him with a strange longing.

Then Wulf looked away north and to his astonishment he thought he could see a little boat, far out and dancing. In a little while, he was sure. And before long, a small egg-shaped craft with a square white sail, almost bouncing on the water, was within shouting distance of the jetty.

Wulf saw there was a single man aboard, waving, and at once he slithered down the steps. He gripped the prow, yanked the rope out of it and pulled it hand over fist until he was holding the tiny boat securely against the side of the steps.

'Ee up, lad,' said the sea-stranger, grinning, and holding out one hand.

'What?' said Wulf.

'I've sailed enough for today.'

So Wulf took his hand and the man stepped out of the boat. Then he rubbed his russet face and

ran his hands through his short dark hair and stretched like a dog.

'Dear bones,' said the man. 'Didst hear them creak, lad?'

'No,' said Wulf. He had never heard anyone talk in such a strange way.

'What's thy name?' said the man. He put a damp hand on Wulf's shoulder and stared at him with his fatherly, grey eyes.

'It's Wulf, then,' said Wulf slowly and carefully.

'Oh aye,' said the man, smiling. 'Th'art no wolf. Th'art some kind creature for helping me so.' Then the man looked about him and sniffed. 'Anyroad, lad,' he said, 'where is't?'

'Where's what?' said Wulf.

'Where is't, lad, this place?'

'Oh!' said Wulf. 'It's the place of giants, by Ythancestir.'

'Ythancestir,' exclaimed the man. 'Christ pre-

8

serve me!' He made the sign of the cross on his chest. 'I was sailing to Rendlesham.'

'Rendlesham,' said Wulf, 'That's where King Æthelhere is.'

'I've come from t'north,' said the man. 'From Northumbria. And t'north wind has driven me too far south.'

'Why are you going to Rendlesham?' asked Wulf.

'To see t'King,' said the man.

'The King!' exclaimed Wulf.

'Aye,' said the man.

'You're wet and cold,' said Wulf. 'Come to the village.'

The sea-stranger nodded.

'What's your name?' asked Wulf.

'Cedd,' the man said. 'Servant of God.'

Then Cedd took down the small white sail and unstepped the mast, and he and Wulf lifted the boat out of the water; Wulf was surprised at how light it was. They carried it just inside the fort and, when Cedd had taken a little leather bag out of it, they turned it over, tipping out such water as it had shipped.

'It's a fair place, is this,' said Cedd, looking around him, nodding at the great stone walls and then stooping to look at the few late flowers gleaming in the grass.

'I often come here,' said Wulf.

'Aye, it's a fair place, this fort o' yours.'

'It is,' said Wulf, rather pleased and proud.

Then together they walked back along the

sandy path to Ythancestir. 'I'll take you to the Earl's hall,' said Wulf. 'Any guest is welcome there.'

Cedd frowned. 'Earl Athulf is it, lad?'

'How did you know that?' said Wulf.

'This is t'third year I've summered with t'East Saxons,' said Cedd, 'spreading the news about Christ.'

'What's that?' said Wulf. '*Christ*.'

Cedd smiled. 'I'll tell thee,' he said. 'Take me to thy own place, not Athulf's hall.'

'My place?' said Wulf.

'Aye,' said Cedd. 'What's good enough for thee is good enough for me. I'll tell thee about Christ then, and tell thy mother and father.'

'Not my father,' said Wulf hurriedly.

'No?' said Cedd, and he turned and looked at Wulf. 'How come lad?'

And Cedd's invitation was so gentle and friendly, that Wulf found himself explaining how his father had been killed in Mercia fighting with Penda against the Northumbrians; how his elder brother Oswald had inherited the family's hide of land; how his mother had swollen eyes . . .

'Oh!' said Wulf, stopping in his tracks.

'What?' said Cedd.

'I forgot,' said Wulf.

He was right. Anna had already seen them approaching, and a moment later Wulf heard his mother trumpeting from inside their hut, 'Wulf! Wulf!'

Cedd smiled at Wulf, as if they shared some

10

secret, and Wulf smiled back and stepped into the hut.

'Wulf,' said his mother. 'The crab! Quick!'

'Mother,' he began.

'I'm going to tear you apart,' said his mother, rising from her straw bed, 'limb from limb.'

At this moment Cedd stepped into the gloom of the hut. 'Peace be in this place,' he said in a firm voice, 'and peace in all who cross t'threshold.'

'Who are you?' said Wulf's mother, brushing pieces of straw from her gown.

'Cedd,' said Cedd, 'servant of God.'

'A Christian?' said the woman.

'Aye,' said Cedd. 'From Northumbria.'

'I've heard your stories . . . '

'I haven't,' said Wulf.

'I've heard your stories, you and your like.'

'Your eyes are swollen,' said Cedd. 'You must bathe them.'

'Athulf the Earl will have none of you,' the woman said. 'Christians are cowards, he says.'

'We fight wi' words, not swords,' said Cedd, smiling. 'But let it be, let it be. Your eyes are swollen; they must be bathed.'

Despite her words, Wulf's mother enjoyed Cedd's concern for her; so Cedd stayed, and himself bathed her eyes, and brought in wood for the fire.

As the day's light failed, Oswald returned to the hut. His blunt fingers were earth-brown, his eyes the colour of ale. It was difficult to believe he and Wulf were branches of the same tree. He was open and Wulf was guarded; Wulf dreamed dreams whereas Oswald believed in nothing he could not see in front of him; to plough straight furrows of earth gave Oswald the same pleasure it gave Wulf to cut and carve straight teeth in his bone comb; Wulf sang and Oswald sang out of tune; Oswald wanted to fight shoulder to shoulder with other East Saxons, and to win fame that would live after him, but Wulf was unhappy at the thought of fighting, screams, smashed shields, heads . . .

Oswald stumped into the hut, nodded at Cedd in a friendly unquestioning way, and without more ado threw himself down in one corner, tired out by the day's work.

'You can stay here if you like,' Wulf's mother said to Cedd. 'Athulf won't entertain you. He doesn't hold with Christians! Isn't that right, Oswald?'

'Uh!' said Oswald.

'Bless thee,' said Cedd. 'Thou'rt as kind as thy son who saved me from t'waves and so forgot his crab.'

Wulf's mother looked at her younger son. 'That's the story, is it?' she said, and she almost smiled.

There was no lack of stories that evening. 'That's the payment a guest must make,' said Wulf's mother, 'a weave of words in return for a bed.' First they ate their fill – rabbit from the pot steaming over the fire, rye bread, sweet water from the well. Then, as Anna curled up in one corner, already drowsy, and the wind wrapped round their hut, Cedd turned to Oswald and asked, 'Ee lad, what dost thou want of this middle-earth?'

'What?' said Oswald.

'What dost thou want to do before thou diest?'

Oswald scratched his head. 'Avenge my father,' he said. 'Avenge him in battle . . . win a name for myself . . . '

'What else?' asked Cedd.

'Isn't that enough?' said Oswald. 'Anyhow, it's in the hands of fate.'

'And thou, Wulf,' said Cedd, 'what dost thou want?'

'I don't know altogether,' said Wulf slowly. 'I know I like carving . . . and singing . . . '

'And dreaming,' Wulf's mother said.

'It depends,' said Wulf.

'On what, lad?' said Cedd.

'Fate,' Wulf replied, shrugging his shoulders. 'It depends on my fate.'

'Does it?' said Cedd.

'What will be,' said Wulf's mother, 'will be.'

'Will it?' said Cedd. 'Listen! A little bird, a sparrow, flies into Earl Athulf's hall. There's feastin' in t'hall. T'poet sits at t'fire, singin' and playin' on t'harp. It's winter outside, storms, rain, hailstones large as grain outside,' said Cedd, 'it's so cold, and it's so warm in t'hall. The little sparrow flies in through one door, into the warmth, and then . . . then it flies out through t'other door. Out into t'night storms again.'

13

'Well?' said Wulf's mother.

'Well,' said Cedd, 'are we like that sparrow? Do we come from t'dark nobody knows about, and live on t'earth – a moment of warmth, a few years of comfort – and then go back into t'dark again?' Cedd paused. 'It's not like that,' he cried. 'There's a life after this one, life in heaven.'

For hour after hour Cedd sat by the glowing fire and told stories and explained how God had created the earth and everything that lives on it, men and beasts, fowls of the air and fish in the sea, and all growing things, great trees and grass blades. He told Wulf and Oswald and their mother about Jesus Christ, and how Christ promised there was an after-life, and died on the Cross to save men.

'It's true, lad,' he said to Oswald, 'fame can live after you. But what's that worth?'

Oswald did not answer.

'What's that worth?' Cedd repeated. 'You talk about a dark world, a world without much 'ope, lad. I talk of a world of light. If you believe in Christ, and try to live as he lived, there's an after-life, a home of happiness. All God's people are there, seated at t'feast for ever and aye.'

Wulf was deeply stirred; his brown eyes were wide with wonder. And his mother and Oswald, too, were moved by what Cedd had to say and the way in which he said it. 'Anyroad,' said Cedd smiling, 'think it out. It's nowt to worry over.'

They lay down to sleep then. But first of all Cedd moved over to Wulf's mother and made the sign of the Cross over her swollen, oozing eyes.

'May the bright eye of Christ behold you,' he said quietly. 'May the hands of Christ heal you.'

The wind sang weird tunes all that night; and then, an hour before dawn, it breathed deeply and fell silent.

A great stillness cradled the sleepers and the hamlet of Ythancestir.

At first light, Wulf and Oswald and Anna, and their mother, and their guest Cedd began to stir in a world between sleeping and waking. Then suddenly they were all awake, stretching, yawning, speaking. Wulf was so refreshed he felt as if he had bathed in a clear pool, and all things seemed possible.

'Mother!' he cried. 'Mother! Your eyes.'

'What?' said Wulf's mother and put her hands to her eyes.

She had no cause to be alarmed. The rims of her eyes had almost entirely healed; they no longer oozed and the terrible swelling had gone. There was only a pinkness to show they had been so badly infected.

'God be praised,' said Cedd.

Wulf's mother looked at him. 'It's fate,' she said. 'Fate! The north wind no longer blows its evil into my eyes.' But secretly she wondered whether Cedd's blessing had anything to do with the cure.

Cedd smiled broadly. 'Fate,' he said slowly, 'aye, fate moves in t'mind of God.'

Then, talking and laughing, the family and

15

Cedd sat down happily together to a meal – rabbit again, and rye bread, and creamy milk that clung to the inside of their mouths.

After they had eaten, Cedd was quick to make his thanks and take his leave. 'Think on what I said to you,' he said. 'I'll come back in God's good time to hear thy answers.'

'I'll come with you now,' said Wulf, almost anxiously. 'Down to the boat.'

'Aye,' said Cedd. 'God bless you all.' And, without more ado, he and Wulf set off down the path that led to the old fort and the sea.

'Cedd,' said Wulf earnestly, 'I won't forget what you said. You know.'

Cedd stopped and considered Wulf.

'What you said last night.'

'Aye,' said Cedd slowly. 'Aye, I know, lad.' He took Wulf's hand and smiled at him long and lovingly. Then Wulf felt so torn inside – so happy, so sad now at Cedd's going.

'I won't forget, you know,' said Wulf.

'I know,' said Cedd gently.

Then they walked on, side by side. And after a while, Wulf asked, 'Why do you have to go?'

'To fight God's fight,' said Cedd.

'Where?' asked Wulf.

'I must go to Rendlesham,' said Cedd. 'But thanks to t'north wind, I met thee; and thou know'st . . . I'll meet thee again.'

'When?' asked Wulf.

'I'll come back in t'spring. I have to see t'King now to ask about preachin' Christ to all the East

Saxons, and ask for a strip of land so I can build. I'll build a cathedral of stone,' said Cedd, tapping the archway of the fort.'

'In the spring?' said Wulf uncertainly.

'That's what I said, lad. Thou'rt my friend, and I'll pay thee a visit. And maybe,' said Cedd, 'maybe, when I come back, thou'll want to be christened with water and become a Christian.'

Wulf nodded. Nothing Cedd said could take away his feeling of sadness. The spring . . . Cedd was going, just as his father had gone . . . Cedd was going and he would be alone again.

'Here, Wulf,' said Cedd, 'I've got a gift for thee.' Cedd rummaged in his leather bag and pulled out of it a slender spoon made of hammered silver. It shone and flashed in the early morning sunlight. Cedd pointed to the word inscribed on its handle.

'Dost thou know what it says?' he asked.

'No,' said Wulf.

'SAULUS,' said Cedd. 'That's what it says. This spoon's one of two – t'first part of a story, you might say.'

'For me?' said Wulf.

'It's thine now, and when I come back . . . '

'You mean . . . ' began Wulf hesitantly.

'Aye,' said Cedd. 'This one's for thee. And when I get back, I'll tell thee t'story about it, and mayhap give thee t'other spoon.'

Wulf had never touched anything so beautiful. He held it between his two hands and marvelled at it. It was finer than the spoons in Earl Athulf's hall.

17

'Now help me with t'curragh, lad,' said Cedd, getting to his feet. So together they carried the little boat back down the landing steps to the sea. Cedd kissed Wulf on the forehead. 'God guard thee,' he said.

'Yes,' said Wulf.

Then Cedd hoisted the sail and the boat was alive on the water. Wulf waved and waved; and for a long while after that he stood at the water gateway, gazing at the blurred white sail, gripping his silver spoon.

2

That was a hard winter. In November, news was brought to Ythancestir of a terrible battle. King Æthelhere joined forces with Penda of Mercia, swearing vengeance on the Northumbrians. A great army of East Saxons marched west and marched north. Few of them marched home again, for the Northumbrians fell on them and slaughtered them on the bank of the River Winwæd in Yorkshire. Penda of Mercia was killed; and Æthelhere of the East Saxons was killed; and thousands of men, loyal to their kings, felt the bite of the sword's edge, and were left after battle as food for the wolf, the raven and the eagle; or else, like Æthelhere himself, they were drowned in the flood waters of the River Winwæd and their bodies were never recovered.

When Wulf and Oswald heard of their King's death, they decided to go to the burial place of kings, near Rendlesham, where a great ship was to be filled with treasures and buried in the King's memory. Cedd may be there, thought Wulf; he told me he was going to see the King. And Wulf all but forgot about Æthelhere and his death for thinking about Cedd . . .

Rendlesham was two days' walk north from Ythancestir, and their mother was against it. But strong-minded as she was, Oswald overrode her, and the two boys made their way across the flat land, through forest and fen, until they came to the burial place.

Wulf soon learned that Cedd had indeed come but had already left for Northumbria; he was bitterly disappointed.

'He left on the first day of the month,' said one grizzled woman. 'The man of peace! And no sooner had he gone than Æthelhere began to gather men to march against the Northumbrians.'

Still, Wulf had little time to brood. He was part of an enormous jostling crowd come to watch as the great funeral ship was hauled up the long slope from the river Deben on pine rollers and, with ropes, lowered into a pit specially dug for it. Everyone marvelled as the waist of the ship was filled with countless treasures in Æthelhere's honour. Men placed there a royal standard and whetstone. Bronze and silver and gold . . . blood-garnets . . . purses full of gold coins . . . brooches, a great buckle . . . bowls, buckets, cauldrons, dishes . . . a horn and a fine harp . . . nobody had ever seen such a treasure hoard.

Wulf was standing at the very edge of the pit, and almost fell in with excitement when he saw two spoons placed in the ship's hold. They looked exactly the same as his own, hidden in a corner of the fort at Ythancestir. Wulf asked the people around him what the spoons were for.

'What do you think?' said one man.

'Eating with,' said another, and his companions guffawed.

But a third man said, 'Those are SAULUS and PAULUS spoons.'

'What are they?' asked Wulf, his heart quickening.

'Christian,' said the man. 'For a Christian before and after he's christened.'

'Why SAULUS?' said Wulf. 'PAULUS?'

'Saulus was a ruler who . . . ' the man hesitated, 'well, he saw the light.'

'What do you mean?' said Wulf.

'He was cruel, he took money from the poor and gave it to the rich. And he had Christ's

21

followers questioned, and tortured, and stoned. But then,' said the man, 'a fierce dazzling light shone on him. He fell down in the road, it was so bright. And he heard a voice coming from that light and asking, "Saul, Saul, why do you torture me?"'

'Who was it?' asked Wulf.

'Well, Cedd said it was the voice of Christ himself, speaking from heaven. That's what Cedd said. Anyhow, that was enough for Saul. He was terrified, and he was blind, too, for three days. After that he became a Christian, and he taught other people about Christ.'

'I see,' said Wulf slowly.

'And he changed his name to Paulus,' said the man, with an air of finality.

'So was Æthelhere a Christian then?' asked Wulf.

'You and your questions!' said the man. 'For a while he was. While Cedd was here, we were all Christians.'

'Well, if he was, why did he go to fight the Christian Northumbrians?' said Wulf.

'Enough!' said the man impatiently. 'He'd sworn vengeance. Christian or not, he had to avenge the death of his kinsmen, didn't he?' And with that the man turned away.

Wulf thought about the story of Saulus, and wished he could hear Cedd explain exactly what it meant. As the great crowd milled about, Wulf stood still and daydreamed. In his mind he turned over all he could remember of Cedd's words, and worried whether he would be able to win an after-life for himself. He thought of the Yule feast in Earl Athulf's hall – heaps of food, horns full of ale, old songs – and wondered whether the feast in heaven would be like that. Rooted to the spot, and looking with a long gaze into the grey shifting skies, Wulf was suffused with the slow warmth of determination. 'I shall be a Christian,' he said under his breath; and then he said it out loud: 'I shall be a Christian.' No one was listening.

The last of the treasures was placed in the ship; then a kind of wooden hut was erected over them and the arduous work began of covering the entire boat and its contents with a huge mound of earth.

'You saw them?' said Oswald.

'What?' asked Wulf.

'All those treasures buried in his honour.' Oswald's eyes were shining. 'For as long as we live, we'll talk of Æthelhere. Fate struck him down, but his name . . . '

'Did *you* see the spoons?' Wulf asked him.

Oswald looked at his brother. 'What are you talking about?' he said. 'Fate struck him down, but his name will live as long as men have tongues.'

At the end of the day, all the women let down their hair and wailed, and twelve warriors mounted on white horses rode round the great mound, chanting words about Æthelhere's life; from time to time the warriors shouted, and from time to time they wept as the women wept. Wulf and Oswald and the whole crowd knelt amongst the trampled bracken, silent and sad.

So darkness fell on the East Saxons. November gave way to December and December to January. Wolves howled in the forest inland from Ythancestir and at night they nosed their way around the little huts. The wind found a way of forcing an entrance everywhere; it cut through clothing, it seemed to enter the body and then the bone itself.

'Time breaks,' said Wulf's mother morosely.

Wulf seldom spoke except when he was spoken to. He sat in one corner of the hut, keeping his thoughts to himself, looking forward to the spring.

3

Spring came, but Cedd did not come.

'He'll come before I've finished carving this spoon,' Wulf said to himself, hacking fiercely at a piece of dumb wood. 'He'll come in the next week, surely.' But still Cedd did not come.

Wulf wandered alone in the old fort. 'He'll come before the primroses die,' he said miserably. He stared at the flowers couched in the new grass, and they looked like pale eyes watching with him for the coming of Cedd.

'He won't come,' Wulf's mother said one morning. 'Why should he?'

'He said he would,' replied Wulf.

'Will, won't, will, won't, will,' said Anna, ticking off her fingers.

'He will,' said Wulf. He always felt unhappy after talking to anyone else about Cedd and so, after a while, he only talked about him to the great comforting stones in his place, the place of giants: 'He said we were friends. He said so. Why hasn't he come?'

From time to time Wulf uncovered the silver spoon he had hidden in the long grass in one corner of the fort. He had wrapped it in a piece of leather so it would not become too tarnished, and whenever he looked at it and held it, he always felt more hopeful, and even asked himself what he would do after Cedd had returned, and how he could be a Christian in more than name.

One morning Wulf was sitting on top of the landing steps outside the north-eastern wall of the fort when he saw a great rowing-boat away to the north, the same kind of boat he had seen at the burial place of kings at Rendlesham. As it came closer, he picked out a purple cross on its sail, and puzzled over its meaning. The sea-steed rode over the waves, and then Wulf saw that it was packed out with men – twenty, perhaps thirty of them. Wulf wondered where the boat could be going, and why. Then, when it seemed almost to have passed the fort, the boat suddenly swung round, its great sail flapping, and headed straight towards him.

Wulf drew in his breath. What could a boatload of warriors want in Ythancestir? He stepped back into the shadow of the great gateway. How could he be sure that they were East Saxons at all? Were they enemies from the north? Should he run to the village?

Before he had time to decide what to do, Wulf heard a clear voice calling out over the shining water; and what he heard over and again was one word, his own name.

'Wulf! Wulf! Wulf!'

Wulf looked, and his heart began to thump painfully.

'Wulf! Wulf!'

Wulf looked again and saw, standing in the prow of the boat, both arms raised . . . 'Cedd!' he yelled. 'Cedd!' And he slithered down the landing steps.

Then the boat eased alongside and even before it was motionless Cedd jumped out and gathered Wulf into his arms.

'Oh!' said Wulf, his voice half-muffled by Cedd's thick mantle. 'I knew you'd come. I thought you wouldn't come.'

'Aye,' said Cedd gently, and hearing him, Wulf knew that he understood everything. He took in a deep breath, and slowly he let it out again. Spring had come late for Wulf; but it had come.

'Wulf,' said Cedd, 'look about thee. Look at my fighting men.'

'Fighting men?'

'Aye, warriors for Christ every one of them.'

Wulf stared at the men disembarking from the boat. Like Cedd, they were all simply dressed in black tunics and black gowns and they wore their hair cut short. But Wulf noticed one difference: while each of them had a small wooden cross dangling round his neck, Cedd wore a cross fashioned with garnets and gold. 'You didn't wear that before,' he said.

'I'm made Bishop of t'East Saxons,' said Cedd smiling. 'And these are my monks to help me preach Christ and teach about t'life after this life.'

'Why did you take so long?' asked Wulf. 'Why couldn't you come before?'

'Ah! Wulf,' said Cedd, shaking his head. 'I've thought often enough o' thee. This spring I had to find thy new King, Æthelwald, and persuade him to become a Christian; and ask his leave to preach Christ to t'East Saxons; and ask for a letter; and beg for a piece o' land to build a cathedral.'

'All those things,' said Wulf.

'Aye,' said Cedd, 'and then back to Northumbria, to report to th'Archbishop. All my talk to Æthelhere last autumn was waste of air.'

'You mean because he died?' asked Wulf.

'Aye, lad,' said Cedd. 'He'd agreed to become a Christian.'

'I know,' said Wulf quickly.

'How's that?' said Cedd.

'I was at Rendlesham,' said Wulf, 'and I saw the SAULUS and PAULUS spoons put in the ship there.'

'Ah!' said Cedd. 'Thou'rt as keen-eyed as a hawk.'

'And I know the story of Saulus,' said Wulf breathlessly.

Cedd smiled broadly at him.

'And I want to be christened,' said Wulf. 'I want to be a Christian. Cedd, I want to be Christian.'

'Wulf, Wulf,' said Cedd tenderly, 'I never doubted thee. From t'day I first set eyes on thee, I knew thou'd want to fight for Christ. To lead a fair life, trying to love thy enemies, slow to anger, quick to forgive.'

'Like you said before,' said Wulf.

'And why shouldst thou wait any longer?' said

Cedd. 'Why shouldst thou wait? Thou'st waited all winter and the best part of t'spring. Where thou leads many another'll follow.'

Then Cedd led Wulf to the water's edge for the christening, watched by all the monks, and asked him to walk into the water, up to his neck, and to duck his head under the water.

'My clothes,' said Wulf.

'As you are,' said Cedd. 'Just as John the Baptist christened Christ in the River Jordan, I'll christen thee.'

So Wulf waded into the water up to his neck, and ducked his head under the water. His fair hair clung to him. Then Cedd signalled to him to return, and when he had waded back to the water's edge, Cedd asked Wulf in front of all the monks if he would try to lead the life of a Christian, a humble life, a loving life, a life fearing God, and Wulf swore to do so. In the

29

peace of that place, under the blue sky dome, Cedd scooped water from the sea and sprinkled a little on Wulf's upturned face and made the sign of the Cross on his forehead. He murmured as bees murmur, 'Mayst thou look upon this child; mayst thou wash him, sanctify him, and may he be delivered from thy wrath. May he pass t'waves of this troublesome world and come at last t'land of everlasting life.'

'Amen,' said the monks.

Wulf was steaming now in the bright sunlight.

'Wulf,' said Cedd, 'we're friends indeed and friends in God. I shall be thy godfather and thou my godson.'

'What does that mean?' asked Wulf.

'It means I must teach thee t'Christian life, and see that thou liv'st it as best I can.' Then Cedd rummaged in his leather pouch and pulled out the gleaming PAULUS spoon and gave it to Wulf. Wulf laughed for sheer happiness and ran at once to the corner of the fort where he had hidden the SAULUS spoon. It had become a little tarnished now.

'Your old dull life,' said Cedd. 'And your new shinin' one.'

'But what am I to do?' asked Wulf. 'What do your monks do?'

Cedd smiled and nodded his head. 'Aye,' he said. 'I understand you. Wait a little, lad, and I'll give thee thy answer.'

Then Cedd and Wulf led the monks to Earl Athulf's hall. Every person in Ythancestir gathered there, and Earl Athulf himself read out King Æthelwald's letter which (just as Cedd had told Wulf) asked them all to listen to the monks and accept Christianity.

But not even Wulf knew how the letter would end; Cedd had kept that a secret. Now Earl Athulf held out the parchment and read:

And I, Æthelwald, by the divine controlling grace King of the East Saxons, have most willingly granted Cedd one hide of land by Ythancestir. If anyone, however – which God forbid – tries to infringe this my grant, let him know that he must render account in the presence of Christ and his angels. This land is the land adjacent to the sea, where in earlier times a fortress stood, of which part still stands . . .

Wulf held his breath. He leaned forward, listening intently.

. . . and I, Æthelwald, have granted Cedd permission to build a cathedral of stone there.

Earl Athulf finished reading, and the hall was filled with talk and argument.

'The cathedral,' said Wulf under his breath. 'In my place.' He felt nervous and excited. So much had happened so quickly that he wanted to be alone. So while everyone was still getting to their feet and the great hall hummed, Wulf ran out and down to the fort. He lay on the sweet grass and began to daydream . . . of who had first built

31

those walls . . . of the secrets he had told those
stones . . . of the father he loved so dearly . . . of
his newfound father in God . . . of that morning,
and the christening. The peace of the place began
to enter Wulf. He was filled with a great slow
pleasure and pride at the thought of the cathedral,
and the knowledge that Cedd would live in
Ythancestir and not go away.

'I knew I'd find thee here,' said Cedd.

Wulf started, and when he saw who it was, he
smiled.

'Dost mind?' asked Cedd, sitting down beside
him.

Wulf shook his head. 'I'm glad,' he said. 'You
won't go away again.'

'Up and down,' said Cedd, 'Up and down,
teachin' Christ to t'East Saxons.'

'I mean you'll always come back.'

Cedd nodded and they sat silent for a while.
'T'best place for my cathedral,' said Cedd conten-
tedly.

'Did you think that when you first saw it?'
asked Wulf.

Cedd smiled. 'Aye, lad,' he said. 'Happen I
did.'

He pulled up a piece of grass and stuck it in his
mouth. 'This is thy place, Wulf,' he said.

'I think that,' said Wulf. 'I've never told anyone,
though. They'd only laugh.'

'It can still be thy place,' said Cedd.

'How do you mean?' asked Wulf.

'Here,' said Cedd, spreading his arms, 'we're

32

going to build t'cathedral and monastery where my monks will live. Each day, in t'church, monks'll pray; they'll sing and pray seven times each day.' Cedd paused and scratched his dark chin. 'But it's like this, lad. In t'monastery, t'monks must bake and brew. They'll grow corn, and thresh and winnow. They'll buy cows, and ewes, and milk them.'

'What do you mean, then?' asked Wulf, frowning. 'How can it still be my place?'

'Listen!' said Cedd. 'At times t'monks will pray, at times they'll take their turn in t'kitchen or farm or t'garden or bakery, and at times they'll go out and preach. But after that, they'll do what they like best to do. One'll string words together . . . one decorate manuscripts . . . one carve bone and stone . . . ' Cedd paused and looked at Wulf. 'And thou, Wulf,' he said slowly and deliberately, 'thou said thou wanted to be a Christian. Canst thou not be one of them?'

'Me?' said Wulf, completely astonished.

'Aye, lad,' said Cedd. 'When I went to t'monastery, I was only seven and thou . . .'

'Eleven,' said Wulf.

'Eleven.'

'But . . .'

'Other boys'll follow thee,' said Cedd. 'I think thou couldst well come, to pray, to help in t'monastery, to carve bone and stone. Oswald looks after thy family's land; there's nowt so much for thee to do at home.' He paused. 'Anyroad,' he said, 'thou'd only be a mile or so from thy mother's place. Thou'd see her and Oswald and Anna day in, day out.'

Wulf looked anxious. He was full of a tangle of thoughts and feelings – wanting to be where Cedd was, wondering about the strange black monks, afraid of what his mother would say.

'Only thou canst decide, lad,' said Cedd gently. 'And not today.'

'No,' said Wulf, grateful for that.

After a while, the two of them walked back to Ythancestir, that huddle of huts and the long hall between the dark fathoms of the forest and the sea. Wulf and Cedd paused outside Earl Athulf's hall, and smiled knowingly at each other as they heard the noise of talk and argument within.

'You know I do *want* to come,' said Wulf.

'I want thee to come,' said Cedd.

'It's just that . . . my mother and Oswald . . .'

'Let it be,' said Cedd as gently as ever, shaking his head. 'Let it be. Like as not, thou'lt have thy answer in t'morning.'

So they grasped each other's hands, friend and friend, Christian and Christian, godfather and godson, and then Wulf went back to his hut, tired out by the day's events and excitements. His mother and Oswald were still in the Earl's hall, but Anna lay asleep in one corner. Wulf lay down beside her, and within a little while he too was asleep.

In Earl Athulf's hall people argued for and against the new Christian faith all night. And at last, when everyone had had his say and some

34

more than once, Earl Athulf and the villagers of Ythancestir decided to accept Christianity and to be christened. The great debate was ended. Wulf's mother and Oswald returned to their hut as the cocks crowed, and at once sank into a deep sleep.

Wulf waited impatiently for them to wake. He wanted to tell them about joining Cedd and his monks; the passing of the night had dissolved his uncertainty, and he was determined nothing should stop him.

When at last they stirred, Wulf first asked his mother and brother to explain what had happened in the hall; then, much encouraged, he told them how he had been christened by Cedd the morning before, and how he wanted to live in the monastery, as Cedd had asked him to do. For once Wulf's mother listened carefully to all her son had to say. She sucked her cheeks thoughtfully.

'You go,' said Oswald. 'You'd never be much of an axe-man.'

Wulf's mother shook her head. 'Christianity till all hours last night,' she growled, 'Christianity this morning.' She yawned prodigiously.

'Jesus Cwist,' said Anna unexpectedly. Her voice was like a treble bell.

'Well! Why not?' said Wulf's mother.

'You know,' said Wulf, 'I will always come to see you here.'

'Why not?' she said again. 'Woden knows, there's nothing for you here. Oswald works the

35

land; and when she grows, Anna will help me.'

'I can go?' asked Wulf.

'You've always been strange; sitting about . . . well, since your father died.' She paused. 'You need a father,' she said.

Then Wulf jumped to his feet and hugged her, hugged her as he had not done for years. And she held him to her with the fierce grip of a bear. 'Wulf,' she said gruffly.

'I'll just go . . . ' said Wulf.

'Tell Cedd,' said his mother.

'Yes, if you're sure.'

'Well, you are!' said his mother.

Then Wulf ran fast and faster. He hurtled down the path to the fort, where he knew Cedd and his monks would be. The sky was pale blue and the grass still heavy with dew. He could hear the sea singing.

'Amen!' he shouted. 'And Amen!'

The Fire-Brother

Almost two years have passed since the missionary Cedd set foot in Ythancestir, blown off course while on his way to Æthelhere's court at Rendlesham. Earl Athulf and the inhabitants of Ythancestir have accepted the new teaching of Christianity, and all been christened, and some of the boys from the village have been taken into the monastery. But the villagers and monks are not finding it at all easy to live side by side, and relations between Wulf and his family are very strained.

It is now the wet summer of 657 . . .

1

'Get away!' said Oswald desperately. As if he were alone on the common land with a dark-eyed bull, and couldn't control it. 'Away! Away!'

But Wulf unhappily stood his ground, staring at his elder brother sprawling against the south wall of their hut.

'Get away!' shouted Oswald, sitting up now, tense and angry. 'What good are you – what good to us or anyone in Ythancestir?'

'We, well, we've built . . . '

' . . . What good is your monastery to us?' said Oswald. 'Tell me that.'

Wulf's mind stammered. He knew there were good answers. If only he could think he would find the words . . .

'Go on!' said Oswald. 'Preach a sermon! That's the only reason you come here each evening.'

'No, no,' said Wulf.

'To warn, to promise and promise, always about heaven and Christ, and . . . '

'Christ!' snorted Wulf's mother. She had dozed off in the hot burst of sunlight that followed the rain of that August afternoon but now Oswald's voice roused her.

'Christ!' she said again. 'You and your Christian monks are free enough with your promises of heaven. But what are you going to do about here and now, Wulf?'

'Now doesn't matter most,' said Wulf. 'Now is soon yesterday.'

'What do you mean?' said his mother. 'What are we going to do this winter, with this terrible harvest, all the corn beaten flat? If we'd sacrificed to Freya, as we used to do, instead of praying to Christ . . . '

Oswald gave Wulf no chance to reply. 'And if the King,' he said, 'had not given a hide of our land to the northern monks.' He shook his head. '*I'm* not your brother. The monks are your brothers.'

Wulf looked at his mother, then at Oswald. 'I come here because I want to come,' he said.

'You're my mother, my brother. Anna's my sister.'

'Leave him alone,' said Wulf's mother before Oswald could bully him further, and then she turned to her younger son. 'Wulf, why don't you come home? Things aren't going well for the Christians, but they're not going well for us either. This is where you belong.'

Wulf turned away to hide the tears that started to his eyes, quite without warning. He knew his only home now was with Cedd and the monks. And as he hurried out from the hut, Anna darted out of it too. She had been trying to hide from the endless quarrelling; now she simply grabbed Wulf's wrist and half-hung on it, slowing him.

Wulf squeezed her left hand and held on to it as they walked past the straggle of huts. They paddled through every puddle on the pocked track.

'I'm five tomorrow,' Anna said.

'I know,' said Wulf.

'I can't wait,' Anna said. 'Can you wait till I'm five?'

'No,' said Wulf, smiling.

'I can't either,' said Anna.

'I've made something for you,' said Wulf.

'What thing?' Anna asked.

'Something,' said Wulf.

Then Anna ran back to her mother and Oswald. Her fair hair jumped up and down on her head as she went. And Wulf took the way out of Ythancestir towards the church and the monastery and the endless sea. He kept thinking about the meetings with his mother and Oswald, how they became more bitter each day, and each time with more accusations levelled at the monks. Cedd should know what my mother said about the harvest, he thought, and what Oswald said about nothing but promises. If only, he thought, I'd found the right answers.

As Wulf approached the great stone church, surrounded by the wooden huts where the monks worked and ate and slept, he heard the bell announcing the service of Compline. He quickened his step and hurried to the boys' end of the monks' dormitory, and there his friends, sons of men in Ythancestir, greeted him.

'Quiet!' said an old monk. 'You know the rule. Silence when the bell begins to toll.'

'You're the cantor tonight,' whispered Edwin

who, like Wulf, was twelve.

'Aidan have mercy!' said Wulf. 'I'd forgotten.'

'You haven't forgotten the psalm, have you?' said Edwin.

'Quiet!' said the old monk.

Wulf grinned at Edwin.

In ones and twos and small knots, all the monks in the monastery at Ythancestir, sixty of them and five boys beside Wulf, made their way to the church. Outside, the day's colours were failing: the sky over the sea was lumpy, a thick purplish grey; and over Ythancestir, in the west, it was streaky lilac and pewter and palest blue. Inside the church the light was both darker and brighter. The walls were shadowy and the lofty roof was shadowy, but the twin altar candles seemed to have set fire to the great gold crucifix between them. And the light from the corona of candles nearby, standing on a pedestal, played among the gold strands in the altar cloth and danced on the gold cross of the man waiting in front of the altar, Cedd, Bishop of the East Saxons, Abbot of Ythancestir.

Cedd saw Wulf come and gestured that, as cantor, he should stand at his left side. Then the shuffling stopped. A stillness grew out of the place and the monks' faces looked white in the dim light. The church smelt of honey.

'May t'Lord Almighty grant us a quiet night,' said Cedd, 'and a perfect end. Brothers,' said the Bishop, 'be loving, be alert. Your enemy, t'devil, goes abaht in many disguises . . . '

43

Wulf was filled with a great comforting warmth. His mind wandered back to that spring morning fifteen months before when Cedd had baptized him on the same spot where the church now stood, amongst the ruins of the old Roman fort. He could hear Cedd saying, 'Wulf, Wulf, I knew thou'd want to fight for Christ. To lead a fair life, trying to love thy enemies, slow to anger, quick to forgive.' Then Wulf thought of Oswald and his mother, how he did love them, and somehow couldn't explain everything to them.

'Glory be to t'Father,' said Cedd, 'and to t'Son: and to t'Holy Ghost.'

Then as the monks responded with one voice, Cedd bent to Wulf and whispered, 'It's thee now.'

Wulf nodded; his heart thumped. And as the reverberation of the monks' voices died away, he began to chant in his clear treble voice:

> *O praise the Lord of heaven: praise him in the height.*
> *Praise him, sun and moon: praise him, all ye stars and light.*
> *Praise the Lord upon earth: ye dragons and all deeps.*

Wulf sang well, balancing the two halves of each verse, articulating each word carefully. He was quite dry-mouthed by the time he reached the end of his great psalm of praise and Cedd resumed, praising God, promising the monks, 'T'parched ground'll become a pool, and t'thirsty land springs of water: in t'habitation of dragons, where each lay, shall be grass, with reeds and rushes.'

Dragons, thought Wulf. Always dragons.

The short service of Compline ended. Cedd asked for peace in the hours of the night and Wulf walked out into the cool darkness.

A strict rule of silence was observed now, and the monks and boys together filed back to the dormitory; their sandals flapped against the wooden boards.

Wulf was restless that night. He moaned a little in his sleep. He turned his head from side to side as if he were trying to escape his own thoughts. Then he began to dream. He was alone in the church with Cedd and he dreamed Cedd was telling him that he must fight the enemy in the forest behind Ythancestir. Then all the monks rushed in and pressed on him a helmet, shouting 'This is the helmet of salvation,' and a shield, shouting 'This is the shield of faith,' and a huge gleaming sword, shouting 'This is the sword of the spirit.' Then Wulf dreamed he went on his way alone. The woods were dark, and the sun – the sky's great candle – only burst through the foliage here and there. He kept tripping. His right forearm ached and he wondered whether he would be able to raise the great sword. So he came to an open place, a glade. At its end stood a mound and there it was, his enemy, it was there! It breathed fire and smoke. Though he could not see it, he could hear it ranting and roaring, and it kept shouting something, the same thing, something he could not quite make out, in a voice he recognized. Wulf wanted to run away, yet thought he had to stay . . .

Wulf woke, damp with sweat and scared. Round him he heard heavy breathing and snoring. He realized where he was: in bed, in the dormitory, his friends around him. For a long time he lay awake, staring into the dark.

Then the monastery bell began to toll. 'Nocturns,' Wulf whispered to himself. 'Seven times a day do I praise thee. At midnight I will rise and give thanks to thee.'

The monks stirred, slipped on their tunics and gowns by the dim light of the single great beeswax candle, and padded away to the church. The boys were excused this one service on the grounds that they were still growing and needed their night's sleep. But Wulf was glad to get away from his nightmare. He dressed quickly and hurried to the church.

Cedd was waiting in that silent, friendly place. He saw Wulf, half-raised his eyebrows, half-smiled.

And so once again, after sleep and before sleep, the monks praised their Maker and prayed for the dove of peace.

2

It was a brilliant morning. There had been more rain during the night, and now the sun used each puddle and wet surface as a reflector. A cool wind blew in off the sea.

Wulf was glad to get out of the dim refectory into the bright light, the more so as there were only a few minutes before the start of Brother Patrick's morning classes. He walked through the enclosure surrounded by the long huts and out of the great gate in the east wall. Unlike the rest of the old fort which had been used for the construction of the church, this wall had been left intact as a windbreak between monastery and sea.

'Cedd!' said Wulf, surprised and delighted.

Cedd looked up from the jetty steps where he was sitting and smiled.

'I mean . . .'

'Thou means, what am I doing here,' said Cedd. 'The same as thee, Wulf.' He stretched out his arms as if he meant to pull down the sun out of the sky.

'I wanted to see you,' said Wulf.

'I don't see thee as often as I might,' said Cedd, shaking his head.

'Well,' said Wulf, 'you've sixty sons here now.'

'Thou'rt chiding me,' said Cedd. And then, direct and concerned as ever, he asked, 'What ails thee, Wulf?'

Wulf looked out to the sea. 'My mother,' he said. 'And Oswald. They ail me. They're against me, and I don't know what to do, or say. Every evening, when I visit them, they complain about the monks here and about Christ Himself, and they curse the day you came and . . .'

'Aye,' said Cedd, raising a hand to restrain Wulf's torrent of words.

But Wulf went on. He described how each meeting with his mother and Oswald seemed worse than the last and he asked Cedd how he should answer them.

'All thou sayest saddens me,' said Cedd. 'Nothing surprises me. Thy mother and brother love thee well enough. It's not just thee on one side and them on t'other. I'll tell thee this: all t'people of Ythancestir are unhappy; their ungrateful mouths are full of complaints and curses.'

'Why?' asked Wulf. 'And what's it got to do with us?'

'This evening,' said Cedd, 'I have to see t'Earl Athulf. We can walk together to Ythancestir, thee and I. And after I've seen him, I'll be able to give thee a better answer.'

Wulf nodded, and looked worried.

'Think!' said Cedd. 'T'people of thy place were quick to accept Christ. 'Appen all too quick.' He paused, and spoke as if he was thinking aloud.

'Tell me, when have t'old folk ever really liked owt that's new? Hast heard St Matthew's saying, "Neither do men put new wine into old bottles"? That's true, is that.'

'You're disappointed,' said Wulf.

Cedd laughed, and ran his right hand through his short black hair. 'No, lad, not disappointed. But impatient. I am that: impatient. Anyroad, let thy mother and Oswald not ail thee. Restrain thy tongue from rough words, thy hand from blows, and thy mind from all harsh thoughts . . .' He looked at Wulf. 'That's not easy.'

'No,' said Wulf.

'Nothing is ever easy in t'kingdom of earth,' said Cedd, smiling. 'Go now, or thou'll be late for Brother Patrick's classes. May t'warm eye of Christ shine upon thee.'

Wulf ran back through the cloisters to the classroom. For a moment he stood outside the door and listened. The first subject of the morning, Latin grammar, had already begun.

'How many genders of nouns are there at all?' he heard Brother Patrick saying.

'Three.' That was Edwin. Or was it Edmund?

'What are they?'

'The first is masculine, as in *hic magister*.'

'What is the second?'

'Feminine, as in *haec musa*. And the third is . . .'

'Wait until I ask you,' said Brother Patrick.

Wulf glanced over his shoulder at the cloisters, and at the roof of the church that seemed to

49

smoulder as the sun dried it, and then he walked into the classroom.

'Wulf,' said Brother Patrick, without waiting for any explanations. 'How many persons of pronouns are there?'

'Three, Brother Patrick.'

'What are they?'

'The first is *ego*.'

'And the second . . . ?'

'Is *tu*.'

'And the third?'

The third is *ille*,' said Wulf.

'Very good. What is the Latin for late?'

'I . . . I don't know.'

'*Tardus*. Why *are* you late?'

'I was talking to Cedd, Brother Patrick.'

'What kind of a Bishop is it at all,' said Brother Patrick, 'that keeps a boy from his classes? And what kind of a monk will you be without knowing your declensions and cases and conjugations? Can you tell me that?'

Wulf smiled.

The hours passed with an arithmetic class and a class in which the six boys practised their writing, each with a stylus and a wax tablet. So the morning ended, and a little before midday the bell began to toll for the office of Prime.

'God help you!' said Brother Patrick, and he dismissed the class with a wave of his small fat hand. 'I doubt if I can.'

The boys went straight from the classroom to the church. Wulf could see Oswald pacing up and down on his strip of land – the nearest to the land belonging to the monastery. He paused and raised his hand to his brother as he had done each day throughout the summer.

Oswald did not wave back. He didn't turn away. He simply stood motionless and watched as Wulf slowly let his arm fall. Then his younger brother was surrounded by a small tide of monks in their black cowls, and they swept Wulf with them into the church.

After Prime the monks gathered in the refectory for the main meal of the day and the boys carried in the food and set it before them – hunks of meat from a freshly slaughtered pig; apples tempting to look at and touch and smell, let alone to taste; and bowls of pale milk from which the cream had been skimmed to make butter and cheese. The monks ate noisily, but in silence, listening or pretending to listen as an old monk read some verses from St Mark's Gospel.

Wulf didn't mind running to and fro with the monks' food before eating his own meal; he didn't mind the rule of silence. Outside these walls, he thought sometimes, people can be against us and against each other, but here in this monastery so little changes; it's the same pattern from day to day.

After the midday meal Wulf went, as he always did, to the monastery workship to carve bone with the old monk, Brother Edward. This workshop was a shed that leaned against the northeast corner of the old fortress; it had no front to it, the clear northern light coursed into it. Here the stones used to build the new church had been squared; here the headstone for Brother Ceorl who died the previous autumn from an adder's bite had been hewn and incised with a cross; here Brother Edward hammered out silver Saulus and Paulus spoons, and the gold chalice that was used in the church had been carefully moulded and decorated with a marvellous design – an inter-weaving of ribbons that seemed to Wulf to have no beginning and no end.

This was the part of the day Wulf like best. He had carved a little casket out of whalebone, and incised a cross on each side of it. Now he was cutting the face of a man on the lid. Brother Edward had promised him that, if it were well done, it could house a relic – perhaps even a piece of St Aidan's mantle – and be placed in the sacrarium in the church. Wulf had been working at it all summer. Day by day he chipped at it, and it was growing. Sometimes he thought the face on the lid had a sort of life of its own and stood back and looked at it, surprised, as if he were seeing it for the first time.

Brother Edward saw that Wulf had a great gift for carving and mostly left him alone. Wulf was grateful for that and knew that whenever he wanted it, Brother Edward would give him advice. So the two of them, the twelve-year-old boy and the old man, worked together in com-panionable silence through the heat of the after-noon. From time to time Brother Edward took a look at the length of the shadows about them, and said at last, 'Time's up, Wulf.'

'Already?' said Wulf, startled.

'You should stop now. Don't forget . . . '

'I haven't,' said Wulf quickly. He put the casket away in the wooden chest at the back of the shed. Then he dipped his hand into his tunic and brought out a small, perfectly cut bone comb.

'Lovely,' said Brother Edward appreciatively.

Wulf laid the comb on the trestle table, placed his fingertips over one end, and with a stylus lightly inscribed four letters on the bar between the upper and lower teeth.

'It's a fair name,' said Brother Edward.

Wulf narrowed his eyes, rubbed at the last letter with the sleeve of his tunic and then inscribed it again.

'You have them straight,' said Brother Edward. 'Five minutes.'

Wulf took a metal spike and scratched the ivory where he had marked it, at first delicately, then with firmer strokes. The bone powdered and Wulf kept blowing it away.

'There,' he said. 'I've done it.'

'It's well done,' said Brother Edward, and he put an arm round Wulf's shoulders. Almost at once the bell began to spell out the minutes before Nones.

After the monks had celebrated the ninth hour, it was time for Wulf to take his turn with milling the flour and, after that, rounding up and milking the cows. And while he was occupied in these ways, his friends and all the monks were at their own appointed duties – one on the monastery land, gathering a sackful of cabbages and one in the steamy kitchen, preparing the evening meal; one shoeing a horse and one sawing wood for a new table in the refectory; one scraping calfskin, removing the blemishes, readying the hide for use in the scriptorium, and one in the scriptorium itself, illuminating a copy of the Gospels with brilliant colours – gold foil, green dye, saffron, and blue dye made from crushed lapis lazuli; one alone in the church decorating the apse with a painting of Christ ascending to heaven; and many more out on the road or in nearby villages, taking medicine to those who were sick, teaching and preaching about Christ. Wherever they went, they tried to leave men happier and more hopeful. Only eighteen months after the cornerstone had been laid, the monastery of Ythancestir, humming with activity, like a great hive, supported itself and gave sweetness to others.

Early that evening, after Vespers and the light meal that followed it, Cedd and Wulf took the straight sandy path that led to Ythancestir. Ahead of them they could see Edmund, Wulf's closest friend, on his way to see his own mother and father. And, as they went, they met several brothers returning late from the more distant hamlets.

'It's a sour summer, is this,' said Cedd.

Wulf tugged at a blade of grass, unsheathed it, and stuck the sweet, succulent root between his teeth.

'Think on this morning,' said Cedd, 'and look at t'sky now.'

Wulf stared at the clouds racing inland.

'They're chasing t'sun,' said Cedd. 'Wolf-clouds, chasing t'sun.' He rubbed his lips together. 'And look at t'corn, lad. If t'people are unhappy, it's nowt to wonder at.'

Either side of the path the patches of corn lay sodden and flattened.

''Appen there'll be enough,' said Cedd. 'It's bad for them and bad for us. We'll scavenge, though, and glean and so get past.'

As they neared Ythancestir, Wulf dragged his feet, thinking of the meeting ahead. 'Will you come,' he said, 'and see my mother and Oswald?'

'Each of us to our own fight,' said Cedd slowly, shaking his head. 'I'll come one time, Wulf, but not tonight.' He smiled at Wulf. 'Remember what I told thee this morning,' he said, and he turned towards Earl Athulf's hall.

A moment later Anna ran out of the hut to greet her brother. Then without more ado Wulf pulled the bone comb out of his tunic pocket and tugged it through Anna's hair.

She yelped, and grabbed the comb, and inspected it.

'It's for you,' said Wulf. 'I made it.'

'I'm five,' said Anna joyfully.

'I know.'

'Could you wait?'

'I couldn't wait,' said Wulf, grinning.

'I'll wear it,' said Anna, sticking the comb back into her hair.'

'It'll fall out,' said Wulf. 'Look!' And he showed Anna her name incised on the flat rib between the two sets of teeth.

'I'm going to show Oswald,' said Anna, and she hared back towards the hut, ahead of Wulf.

Oswald was standing in front of the entrance as if he were defending it. He took no notice at all of Anna who tugged at his sleeve but, as Wulf drew near, he spat deliberately in front of him.

Wulf's heart pumped uncomfortably.

'Get away!' said Oswald in a low voice.

That scared Anna and she ran off to find her mother and show her the comb that Wulf had made for her. Wulf forced himself to look at his brother and saw his eyes were blazing.

'You've moved my markers,' said Oswald.

'What?' said Wulf, astonished.

'You heard: you've moved my markers.'

'Where?'

'The two nearest the monastery. You've stolen six paces of my land.'

'Oswald!' exclaimed Wulf. 'How could you?'

Oswald looked at the ground.

'Me!' said Wulf. 'Stealing *your* land?'

'Get away!' snarled Oswald.

Then Wulf suddenly remembered his dream of the night before, the journey he did not want to make, the repeated words. Over the forest, away west, clouds were gathering and bleeding.

'You,' said Oswald. 'Or one of your monks. You've stolen my land.'

'No!' cried Wulf angrily.

'What the monks weren't given, they thieve inch by inch.'

'That's not true,' said Wulf.

'Where will it end?' shouted Oswald.

'It's untrue,' protested Wulf. 'You know it is.'

Oswald spat again. 'Where will it end? You tell us not to make boasts but pray; you tell us not to throw spears but sing psalms; you take our land.'

'No monk in the monastery would ever steal land,' shouted Wulf, more angry and upset than he had ever been before.

'You and your monks,' Oswald sneered. 'We'll use our pitchforks. We'll use our forks and pitch you all into the sea.'

'Liar!' shouted Wulf. 'Liar! Liar!' He heard himself shouting louder and louder.

Then, quite suddenly, Oswald turned and slouched off, muttering something. Wulf looked at him, amazed. He had stood firm and Oswald had backed down; it had never been that way before. But now? Now all Wulf wanted to do was sob.

That was an end to it. Wulf didn't want to go, but he could barely stay. Without seeing his sister again, and without seeing his mother at all, he turned away and hurried out of the hamlet back towards the monastery.

Wulf went over that violent argument time and again, and felt a pressing pain in his chest. He didn't see how things could ever get better between him and his brother. The wind swirled and skirled around him.

'Lighten our darkness,' cried Cedd. 'And by thy great mercy defend us from all perils and dangers of this night; for t'love of Thy only Son our Saviour Jesus Christ.'

The office of Compline ended then. But Cedd did not bless and dismiss the monks with the sign of the cross. Instead, he asked them to remain where they stood and, himself standing beside the altar, said, 'Brothers, we're surrounded by dangers and darkness. Many men about us wish us ill, men of little faith and less forgiving.' Cedd paused; nobody moved. 'This afternoon, I saw t'Earl Athulf. He told me his people were blaming us for t'wind and rain, and t'wrecking of harvest.' He paused again. 'Have you heard talk of that?'

A number of the monks nodded and murmured.

'T'Earl says that since they deserted Freya for Christ, they've had more foul days than fine.' Cedd threw back his head. 'As if an idol could change t'weather,' he said contemptuously. 'But that's not all. He said we strip families of sons against their will. That's not so. He said we take food out of t'mouths of his people. But that's not so either; the land we work was given to us by t'King and never worked before. He said we shelter wandering men exiled from their own homes. At times that is so; it's not right any man under heaven should starve or freeze. And he said our cows have twice strayed and eaten off the common land. If that is so, we must be more careful.' Cedd looked about him. 'And lastly, t'Earl said we stand accused of moving land markers.'

Several monks murmured angrily, and Wulf shook his head fiercely.

'I'm quite sure that is not so,' said Cedd. He fingered the gleaming cross that hung round his neck. 'I answered t'Earl as I've spoken to you. And I told him, too, that we've come here to give and help and warn and love, as Christ tells us; we've not come to take or wrong or damage in any way.' Cedd, it seemed, half-smiled. 'Brothers,' he went on, 'it's a bad harvest, and t'people fear t'wolf of winter. And they're afraid of our ways. Men often fear what they do not fully understand. They're angry and unhappy; do not make them more so.'

Wulf peered about the church. The figures of the monks cast giant blurred shadows on the roof and the walls, as do moving clouds over green fields and fields of corn.

'If you're struck on one cheek, turn t'other,' said Cedd. 'It's not easy; I never pretended that.' He shook his head, and spoke quietly now as a pigeon at nightfall. 'Be peaceful. Let time pass and t'anger of those against us will pass too. Be peaceful this night.'

Then Cedd made the sign of the cross, and the monks drifted out into the summer night. Wulf walked sedately back to the dormitory, carrying Cedd's words and warnings with him. It took him less time to get to sleep than he expected.

3

The fine weather came too late. The benign sun and cloudless skies mocked the villagers as they reaped the remains of their harvest. Side by side with the monks, they sullenly cut their corn, and their women followed after them, gleaning the ears that survived the gleaming scythes.

Wulf's mother said every man and woman and child would go short that winter. 'That's our fate,' she said. 'And one way or another the monks will pay for it,' she warned Wulf darkly. 'That will be their fate.'

After the reaping, the stubble was fired. More than twenty small strips of flame flickered and prospered in the dry last days of summer. Blue smoke wove patterns like rising mist. The sight of it and thick smell of it delighted Wulf. At times the smoke thinned until he could only tell it was still in the air because the land behind it – the huts and the forest – seemed to tremble. Then heaven swallowed the smoke.

Wulf was out on the edge of the monastery land, alone with the cattle, when he saw it happen. It was the end of a smouldering afternoon and all the monks were in the church arguing (not for the first time) over the date of Easter. It happened so suddenly.

Wulf saw a figure running from the strip of land nearest to the monastery, running towards the monastery, carrying a bundle of burning stubble. It was only two hundred yards. He was there, he was holding up the flickering flames to the thatched roof of the nearest hut, the infirmary.

Wulf was on his feet and shouting and tearing towards the church. 'Stop!' he yelled. 'Stop! Stop!'

He was too late. Greedy tongues of flame were licking the straw roofs of the wooden huts and nothing could have saved them. Wulf threw open the doors of the church, still shouting, and the monks streamed out. But the infirmary was already crackling and spitting; it was a terrifying throat of fire.

Then Cedd gave order after order. The monks ran to the refectory, the kitchen, the dormitory, the library, the scriptorium, the sculptorium, and came staggering back with whatever they could carry – books, clothing, skins, drinking horns, bellows, half-carved wood and bone and stone, silver ware, tablets of wax. They placed them all in the cool sanctuary of the stone church, and then they turned again and, in twos and threes, coughing and spitting the acrid smoke out of their lungs, they carried out chests and pallets and trestle tables wherever the fire and smoke did not already prevent them. Like a tide the flames flowed from building to building, withering in seconds and minutes what had taken months and years to grow.

When the monks could no longer withstand the heat, and there was nothing more they could do, several of them buried their smudged faces in their hands, unable to look at the burning monastery. Only Wulf stood quite apart, knowing and desperate. He watched roof-beams crack and collapse, and whole walls fall flat, and heard the angry spitting and the voice of the fire. The light wind fanned the flames, leading them first in one direction, then in another. That was a terrible sight.

Then Cedd asked all the monks to go into the church. Sooty and shaken, but all of them alive and unscathed, they filed slowly into that silent lofty place. Flames lapped around the outside of the stone apse; they could not unmake it.

Cedd himself walked over to Wulf. He understood him so well that, the moment he saw him, he could tell what had happened. He put an arm round Wulf's shoulders. They stood like that for a moment, the two of them, as once they had stood in that same place, sharing a dream. Then Cedd looked earnestly at Wulf and Wulf, his eyes burning with shame, bowed his head. 'Yes,' he said in a low fearful voice.

'Aye,' said Cedd slowly, and very sadly.

'Oh Cedd!' said Wulf, and suddenly he felt tearful. He screwed up his eyes and rubbed his eyelids.

'Thou'rt sure,' said Cedd.

Wulf said, 'I saw him.'

'T'waste,' cried Cedd in anger. 'T'waste.' Then he took a deep breath and thought for a while. 'I've a charge for thee, Wulf,' he said at length. 'What's worse? To have everything except love? Or have love but nothing else?'

'We, we . . . ' stammered Wulf.

'What we've lost we must rebuild,' said Cedd. 'Anything man makes can be remade. But thou hast not lost thy love, and thou must not lose it. I know thou loves him. Go and comfort him, wherever he is.'

'I can't,' said Wulf in a strangled voice.

'He'll not come back to t'village otherwise. How could he, fearing vengeance as he will?'

Wulf looked afraid.

'Tell him our ways are not his ways. Tell him there'll be nowt to answer for, and no one to answer to except himself. We've no feuds here.'

'He won't understand.'

'That's thy charge,' said Cedd. 'Go while t'sun is still high.'

Wulf ran the whole way to Ythancestir. His long strides ate up the sandy track. He thought of himself running, and felt the pounding of his feet, he side-stepped, jumped over pot-holes, gasped for air, all he thought of was running for fear of what lay behind him, and what lay ahead.

Wulf went first to his mother's hut. She was sitting outside it in the sunlight, plucking a chicken. Anna was making a maze beside her.

'Oswald,' gasped Wulf. 'Is he here?'

64

'Uh?' grunted his mother.

'Oswald. Where is he?'

'I don't know.' She shrugged her shoulders. 'What's that fire at the monastery?'

'You haven't seen him?'

'Why?'

Wulf looked into the dark hut; it was empty. 'The monastery, the whole monastery's burnt,' he said, and pointed to the eastern skyline where a great column of smoke was spreading out and feathering. 'And, and, Oswald . . . '

Wulf's mother looked seriously at her younger son; then she averted her gaze from him.

'What?' said Anna. 'What did Oswald do?'

'He did,' said Wulf. 'I saw him.'

'No,' said Wulf's mother, and her voice broke with uncertainty. 'He wouldn't do that,' she said. 'Not your brother. He wouldn't do that.'

'I saw him,' Wulf repeated.

'What did Oswald do?' asked Anna again.

Wulf looked forlornly at her, and ran one hand through her hair. 'I must find him,' he said. 'I must.'

It was the same at Athulf's hall; no one had seen Oswald since he had gone to his plot of land after the meal at midday. The Earl himself listened and told Wulf, 'Find him! Let him speak for himself! If what you say is true, he'll never step again on his own land; and no one here will shelter him.'

'He hasn't harmed you,' said Wulf.

'Our ways are different from yours,' said

Athulf. 'But whether we like it or not, we must learn to live together.'

'My lord,' said Wulf. 'If Cedd the Bishop and the monks forgive him, you could forgive him too.'

Then Wulf left the hall. He wondered where Oswald would have gone first and decided that

he must have run on from the monastery into the
cover of the scrub and the trees that came down
almost to the water's edge. And then, thought
Wulf, if he wanted to get right away, he would
have made inland and rejoined the forest track
somewhere beyond Ythancestir.

So Wulf took the inland track out of the hamlet,

wishing he did not have to go into the forest with no hope of getting through it before nightfall. He did not run now, there was no point in that. As he walked, he thought of what Cedd might have said to the monks in the church after he had gone; and how the monks would be scavenging in the ashes for their possessions; how the cattle, the slow, dependable, comforting cows would still have to be milked, fire or no fire. Wulf's mind ranged back and forward: he thought how he wanted and did not want to find Oswald; how once, and not since then, they had together taken this same track, hurrying to the great ship burial at Sutton Hoo. He thought of the dream-dragon in the forest.

The sun dropped and the shadows grew darker. The shapes of the tree trunks did not reassure Wulf: he kept looking at them in case one of them did move and jump as so many of them threatened to do. It was almost night when Wulf saw some way ahead of him a little fire by the side of the track. At once he left the path for the trees and padded in an arc over the soft leaf-mould, nearer and nearer to the fire, and the figure sitting beside it. He peered. He inched closer, and peered again, anxious that even a breaking twig might give his presence away. A man was sitting with his back to him, cutting up meat, too busy with that to notice anything else.

Wulf peered again. He was close enough now; he was sure. 'Oswald!' he called in a loud, clear voice.

Oswald leaped to his feet, his knife in his hand.

'Oswald, it's me, it's only me.'

'Get away!' said Oswald, baring his teeth.

'No,' said Wulf, and he boldly stepped into the small pool of light surrounding the fire.

'Who's here? Who's with you?'

'No one.' Wulf shook his head. 'No one.'

Oswald stared into the almost-darkness behind Wulf.

'That meat looks good,' said Wulf.

Oswald stepped towards the trees behind Wulf, raising his knife. Nothing moved. He turned back towards Wulf, who had dropped on one knee beside the fire, and was staring into it.

A large bird got up nearby and Oswald was on his guard again. It flapped heavily away, leaving the two of them to the night silence.

'Oh! Oswald,' said Wulf.

'Everyone hates the monks,' said Oswald. 'I did what everyone wants to do.'

'Do they?' said Wulf. He thought for a while; Cedd's words about love came back into his mind, and he was filled with a great relief at having found Oswald. 'All the monastery's burned,' he said, 'all except the church.' Then without reproach, he sadly described to Oswald, as if he were his dearest friend, everything that had happened – how the monks had lost the buildings they had taken more than a year to erect, and lost more of their possessions than they had saved. Oswald sat and listened until Wulf stopped to collect his thoughts again.

'So why did you come?' asked Oswald.

'I don't know,' said Wulf. 'We're brothers, aren't we?'

'I don't understand you.'

'Perhaps you don't,' said Wulf.

'They'll be after me in the morning,' Oswald said.

'No.'

'They will. They'll want vengeance.'

'No,' said Wulf again. 'They won't. Not the monks.'

'I know how things are. Before morning I must leave Ythancestir far behind me . . . '

'No,' said Wulf a third time, his voice rising.

' . . . and find some place – some lord who knows nothing of my history.'

Wulf shook his head. 'Your way is not the way of exile,' he said.

'I know how things are,' said Oswald fiercely.

'You know how things are between kings and earls and freemen,' said Wulf, needing and finding the right words and arguments. 'That's not how they are between monks.'

'If the monks had never come, this would never have happened,' retorted Oswald.

'The monks want you to come back.'

'Come back?' yelped Oswald.

'Come back to where you were born, and where you belong.'

'No,' said Oswald.

'Cedd said so,' continued Wulf. 'And the Earl said we must learn to live together.'

'No,' said Oswald again.

'This is how the Christians are. They don't want vengeance. They're sad and angry, but they don't want any feud. If you come back, Oswald, I give you my word . . . '

Oswald sat motionless.

'Our mother and Anna, what will they do without you? Who would work the land?'

Oswald shrugged his shoulders.

'I know you don't like the monks, but at least they're forgiving . . . I know you don't like me since . . . '

'It's nothing against you,' said Oswald.

'If you come,' said Wulf, 'we'd be a kind of cornerstone . . . '

'You!' scoffed Oswald. And he leaned over and punched Wulf in the ribs as he so often used to do when they were both younger, two brothers under one roof.

'Well,' said Wulf excitedly, 'So will you?'

'You were always like that,' said Oswald. 'Dreams!'

'You'll come,' said Wulf. 'You'll come, won't you?'

'I'm hungry,' said Oswald. Then together the two brothers cooked and ate the chunks of meat Oswald had been preparing when Wulf had first seen him.

'Shall we go now?' said Wulf anxiously, feeling that, now the meal had ended, in some strange way his brother was already drifting away from him again.

Oswald shook his head.

'Why not? Why?'

'I don't know,' said Oswald, and his voice was stone-cold. 'I want to think.'

'Let's go now,' said Wulf.

Again Oswald shook his head.

Then Wulf stood up, and stretched. For a moment he bore down on Oswald's shoulders with both hands.

'You will come,' he said. 'I know you'll come.'

Then Wulf stepped out of the fire-circle, and away into the darkness. He had done all he could and with all his heart hoped it was enough. He suddenly felt so tired, terribly tired, and he wanted to be back with Cedd and the monks.

Wulf walked and walked and at last the forest opened and receded. Ahead lay nothing but silent Ythancestir, then the gutted monastery and the restless, rocking sea.

Wulf heard himself chanting a line from the psalm. 'In the habitation of dragons, where each lay, shall be grass, with reeds and rushes.' He was dazed with effort and tiredness, and couldn't think why the words should have come into his mind.

Just then, and Wulf found it quite wonderful, the distant voice of the great church bell began to toll.

Like a promise, thought Wulf. A kind of promise. And he hurried on through the sleeping hamlet.

And Oswald, he too probably crept back to his place there later that same night.

The Earth-Father

Oswald's action in setting fire to the monastery has had the effect of bringing the monks and villagers much closer together. They have buried their differences and all (including Oswald) rebuilt the monastery together.

Almost two more years have passed. Wulf is now fourteen, and it is the early spring of 659.

1

'Your legs are too long for your body,' panted Brother Patrick. 'So they are.'

Wulf grinned. 'Yours are too short,' he said.

'Ah! They're poor creatures,' said Brother Patrick sorrowfully.

The pair of them were on their way back to the monastery at Ythancestir, and a comic enough sight they made, Wulf lean and lanky, Brother Patrick tumbled out of some pudding mould, as they hurried along under the threatening March sky. That afternoon it had been almost hot, and they had actually broken sweat as they laboured to teach the Creed to a group of villagers at a nearby hamlet.

'Men made that prayer too long,' said Brother Patrick.

'They did,' agreed Wulf.

'Like your legs,' Brother Patrick said. 'Too long altogether.'

But now it was customary March again. At the end of the day, there was more of winter past than summer to come in the air.

In Ythancestir itself there was nobody about.
All the villagers had been summoned by Earl
Athulf to swear to the service they owed him: the
number of days they would work on his land, the
rent of pence to be paid at Midsummer, the
sesters of barley and the number of hens they
would hand over at the autumn solstice.

Wulf was glad he was part of the community of

monks, where each worked for all, and all for God. The monastery seemed to him a happier, more hopeful place than the huddle of huts where he had been born and first brought up. He peered into the ramshackle hut where his mother and Oswald and Anna lived. 'No,' he said. 'No one.'

'Put a halter on your ankles, won't you?' said Brother Patrick.

'Look at that!' exclaimed Wulf, pointing down the straight track ahead of them.

At its end, a mile off, exposed to whatever the

elements might throw at it, stood the mighty
church. The rebuilt wooden huts clustered at its
foot. Around it, windswept fields, brown and
green-grey; beyond it, a sombre strip – that was
the sea; and above it, angry clouds, clouds that
meant rain and more rain. And yet, as fate had it,
there was a fissure in the lighter clouds inland to
the west, and the early evening sun poured
through it. One great shaft irradiated Cedd's
church. The stone shone soft and inviting, the
yellow of richest butter.

'It's something wonderful,' said Brother Patrick.

Wulf nodded. The two of them stopped and stood, awestruck by the sheer beauty of it.

Then the fissure closed like an eyelid. The first heavy drops began to fall, soon quickening and settling into determined rain.

'Come on!' said Wulf.

Brother Patrick plodded down the track behind Wulf. 'That beam,' he said. 'Such a thing never happens by chance.'

'I wish Cedd were back,' Wulf called over his shoulder. 'He would have liked that.'

'Ach! He'll be back soon enough,' said Brother Patrick. 'That Bishop is always coming and going. North to Bishop Finan at Lindisfarne, south to Tilbury, north again to Lastingham; he fathers monasteries like some men father children! Ah! But when the Bishop's away, I'm happy enough myself under Brother Wilfred. He'll make a good Abbot one day, and that's for sure.' Brother Patrick was back in full voice now as the two of them resigned themselves to a drenching, and slopped slowly back towards the monastery.

That was not the best of days. Shortly after Wulf and Brother Patrick had exchanged their satu-rated clothes for dry ones, a small currach came in and anchored at the monastery jetty. There were two monks in it and, bedraggled and frozen as they were, they asked to speak at once with Brother Wilfred.

But even before they could be led to him, the terrible news the monks had brought was on their tongues. They said they came from Cedd's monastery at Lastingham; they said the plague had struck there and that many were dead, more dying. And they said that Cedd, after nursing the stricken brothers day and night, had himself caught the plague and lay there, sick, if he was not dead already.

Some of the monks wept openly. Others ran about taking the news to those who had not heard it. Wulf went alone to the deserted church; he knelt on the flagstones before the gleaming altar cross, but even before he could order his teeming thoughts and pray as Cedd had taught him to do, another monk burst in to ring the bell. Soon the lofty church was filled with faces pallid in the gloom.

Brother Wilfred lost no time. He asked the two monks from Lastingham to tell the assembly everything they knew; but that was no more than the little they had already said, except that Cedd had reminded his brothers at Ythancestir that it was all but three years since he had first come south to that place, and asked them to continue his work there whether he lived or died.

Tears sprang to Wulf's eyes.

'Our father is in God's hands,' said Brother Wilfred. 'As we all are.' He fingered his beard nervously. 'Understand this. Bishop Cedd may yet live . . .'

And he may die, thought Wulf. He could think

that thought, but he couldn't think beyond it. He felt as if he were facing a high wall he didn't know how to climb over.

'We can only pray,' said Brother Wilfred.

'We can go to him if we want to,' Wulf heard himself say. He heard himself calling out the words, loud and clear, as if he were outside his own body and listening to another person. And then he heard all the monks begin to murmur.

Brother Wilfred waited in vain for the disturbance to subside. He raised both hands but the voices became more insistent. He called out then, 'Brothers!' And then louder, 'Brothers! Wulf's not right to speak out of turn. And yet he is right. We can go to Cedd. Those who want can go north to be with Cedd.'

There was a great hubbub then, and it became clear that Wulf had spoken for half the monastery. Later, each monk in turn prayed aloud for Cedd's recovery; and in the end it was decided that no fewer than thirty of the monks, taking Wulf with them, would leave next day for Lastingham.

2

The routine of the monastery was suspended. At first light the church bell was rung simply to wake the monks and not to summon them to Matins. Wulf threw on his tunic and mantle, ate hunks of bread and cheese and drank his fill of milk in the refectory, and then hurried off to Ythancestir to tell his family of his intended journey.

In fact, Wulf arrived so early that his mother and brother and sister were only on the point of beginning their own meal. 'Cedd has the terrible plague,' Wulf said, answering their upturned faces.

'Not here?' said Oswald, alarmed.

'In Lastingham.'

Oswald frowned.

'I've told you before,' said Wulf. 'That's his monastery in Deira.'

Wulf's mother made the sign of the Cross and, looking at her younger son, she shook her head and sighed. 'Only fools complain at fate,' she said.

'I've come up to tell you I'm going north, straight away,' said Wulf.

Wulf's mother got to her feet.

'With thirty monks,' said Wulf. 'We want to be with Cedd.'

'When are you coming back?' asked Anna anxiously, trying to piece together what she had heard, and sure only that Wulf was going away.

Wulf ruffled his sister's pale gold hair. 'Soon, Anna,' he said. 'Pretty soon.'

'Wulf,' said his mother in a low voice. 'You cannot, cannot go.'

'I must,' said Wulf with a simple conviction.

'You'll not come back,' said Oswald.

'I remember the last time here,' said Wulf's mother grimly. 'The plague year, that was the year we married. Everyone was so afraid.' She paused. 'Three out of every four ... Three out of four! Can you imagine?'

'Soon,' said Anna.

'Deira,' Oswald said darkly. 'The men of Deira killed our father.'

'Oswald!' protested Wulf.

'You know they did,' said Oswald. 'He marched north with the Mercians and the men of Deira killed him.'

'I'm going because of Cedd,' insisted Wulf.

'I'll have nothing to do with them,' said Oswald, 'except when the time for vengeance comes.'

'I venerate our father too,' said Wulf. 'As much as you do, I do. There's no day I don't think of him.'

'You never ask about him,' said Wulf's mother morosely.

Wulf closed his eyes and bit his lower lip. 'I think about him,' he said, remembering the many, many days when he had confided secret memories of his father to the silent stones in the ruined fort, recalling the way in which he sometimes muddled memories of his father with his thoughts about Cedd. 'But that fight's not my fight,' he said. 'What use is vengeance? And what's the use of endless memories?'

'They're a dead man's life,' said Oswald.

'You say you're Christian,' retorted Wulf, 'and you talk of vengeance. Anyhow, the East Saxons are Christians now and the people of Deira are Christian. No harm will come to me there.'

'Nor to them, it seems,' snapped Oswald.

They talked a little longer. But the more words that passed between them, the more it became clear that Wulf had made up his mind and that nothing on this middle-earth would change it. Wulf's mother put her head between her hands, and Oswald rubbed his unshaven chin.

Unable to understand the argument, Anna's mind had travelled off on a journey of its own. 'Are there bedgebogs where you're going?' she asked unexpectedly.

That made them all smile, despite themselves.

'Bedgebogs,' said Wulf. 'Well, if there are, I'll bring you one. With more spikes than teeth in a comb.'

Then he embraced each of them. Wulf's mother was more upset than she had been since his father's death. She clung to Wulf fiercely.

'I'll say a charm for you,' said Oswald.

Wulf smiled, and was gone; he made his way out of the hamlet, and back to the monastery.

The boat in which Cedd's monks had first come south, and which had been used very little since that time, was moored to the fort's old stone jetty. The water slapped and sucked at the steps, anxious for the boat to begin its journey.

So were the monks, though the two men who had brought the news from Lastingham decided to stay at Ythancestir and rest for a while. The travellers stowed away everything they needed to take with them: clothing, great panniers of food and earthenware jugs of milk and water. But that was not all. Old Brother Edward, the carver, brought pieces of bone and several knives and a whetstone; Brother Oswiu brought his lyre; Brother Patrick a gospel-book borrowed from the library. The monks were taking so much that Wulf wondered whether they ever intended to return.

Well before midday the thirty monks were prepared, and they all embarked, twenty of them sitting to their oars. Brother Wilfred, whose duty it was to stay behind and care for the monastery, called on God to bless his brothers and protect them from harm, and himself cast them off.

That boat was a proud sight, a sea-steed riding over the waves, with Brother Anselm, the helms-man, sitting in the stern.

Wulf had been out on the water before, but only in a currach. At first he was alarmed by the irregular way in which the boat surged forward and lurched and dipped, seeming to take his stomach with it, but he was surprised and pleased to find he could stand up, legs apart, and even warily shuffle around. Nothing, though, excited him as much as the hoisting of the sail, the great sea-garment. It rustled as it was unrolled and flapped as it was hoisted, then beat like a single, great, violent wing.

Then the boat ran north before the wind. The oarsmen shipped their oars and left their seats; they rubbed their red hands, ready to eat. And soon their thoughts turned to Cedd once more.

'How long will we be?' asked Wulf.

'Two days,' said Brother Anselm, signalling to Wulf to sit down beside him and putting his hand on the quivering steering paddle. 'No more if God gives us these good winds. Two days to the

monastery at Whitby, and a day's walk from there to Lastingham.'

The only time Wulf had ever travelled far from Ythancestir was when he walked with Oswald to Rendlesham. As the afternoon grew long, the brilliant islands of sunlight on the water, the smell of tar, the tang and taste of salt, the sound of the water always sluicing under the keel and slopping against the ribs of the boat under the gunwales, the very feel of the surging boat – they all began to weary and oppress Wulf. He had a dull ache in his head.

So that sea-passage continued. The monks gave their Maker thanks for the sunlight and the full moonlight and sailed north, first past Caister, then north-west to the mouth of the Humber, and from there to Kilnsea. They ate, they huddled together for warmth, they dozed, they sang psalms, they prayed for Cedd, and always one of them steered and another kept watch in the prow. So at last they rounded the hook of Flamborough Head and in the afternoon of the second day, they anchored and disembarked at the monastery of Whitby.

For some time Wulf could not get used to the ground once more beneath his feet. It didn't feel steady; it seemed to heave. Wulf felt strangely dizzy too, as if he had drunk too much mead.

The salt-stained travellers were eagerly welcomed by their fellow monks at Whitby. 'New faces!' said one monk, as if he were describing some miracle. 'Our doors are closed,' said another as he led them into the monastery, 'except to seafarers. We've had to bolt them against the plague.'

Then the monks were greeted by Abbess Hild herself. They explained why they had come, and she told them the plague was raging at Lastingham and a dozen other Northumbrian monasteries besides. She praised them all because their love for Cedd was greater than their fear, but then she warned them: 'If you come back, bring enough food to last until you're home in Ythancestir. We cannot open our doors to you. Cedd's brothers are there already,' said the Abbess. 'Cynebil and Cælin and Chad . . . they came this way four days ago.'

In the morning, the monks were up early. They celebrated the office of Matins at first light, they ate and drank, and then they left Whitby; the monks there wished them God's speed and His protection.

It was a walk of twenty miles to Lastingham. As they turned away from the sea, and climbed the track that struck inland, Wulf was astonished at the sheer size of the hills. He had always thought of the middle-earth as almost flat.

'Not at all,' panted Brother Patrick, who was already finding it difficult to keep up with the eager pace set by the younger monks. 'The world's full of mountains. I've surely taught you that.'

Wulf felt a tremendous surge of excitement as he strode along a great ridge; the land fell away to either side, and he saw untamed pastures rippling around him, where only sheep strayed. 'Glory be to God!' he shouted, and the wind whipped the words out of his mouth.

For two hours the monks followed the course of a bubbling river, then, as they had been instructed, they took a little-used track away to the south-west. The day's first brightness had gone, and the sky was strait-jacketed. Wulf looked at the steep grey-green slopes to left and right, the harsh outcrops of rock, and the uninviting lonely valley ahead, and for a second time on the journey he felt oppressed. He wondered whether it was right to have come and he knew it was far too late to turn back.

The monks, however, moved resolutely forward; and as they walked, they sang:

The Lord is my shepherd . . .
Though I walk through the valley of the shadow
of death, I will fear no evil . . .

As the hours passed, Wulf felt in a strange detached mood, and thought perhaps it didn't really matter what happened after he reached the monastery at Lastingham; what mattered was not whether Cedd died or he died or any of the monks died, but, rather, their living care for each other.

The last five miles were the roughest – across wind-blasted hill country, tricked out with treacherous peat bogs, where the bones of the earth were everywhere bursting through its skin. Wulf scratched his weary legs on the rough heather and grazed one knee when he tripped and stumbled over a rock.

Then, late in the afternoon, the land in front of them began to fall away, and below them the monks saw a hollow in the moors. It was very green, a fertile place watered by a beck, protected from the winds, tended by men's hands. And on the opposite bank stood an austere cluster of buildings: a grey stone church, grey wooden buildings beside it, and a handful of huts scattered around.

'Look at that!' said Brother Patrick with evident satisfaction. 'Isn't it as fine a place as you could wish to see?'

'Cedd told me once,' said Wulf, 'that Lastingham looked more like a lurking place for
robbers and retreat for wild beasts than like a
habitation for men.'

'True enough, the way we've come,' said Brother Patrick. 'But this valley is beautiful.'

Wulf stared down at the buildings.

'Look!' said Brother Patrick.

A man had come out of one of the huts opposite. He waved to the monks and bawled 'Plague!
Plague!' The place took up his call, and his voice
echoed eerily – Plague, Plaiegue, Plaieegue, Plaiee
– as it rebounded from escarpment to escarpment.

The monks, grouped closely together now, walked steadily forward. They passed two bodies,
still unburied, lying side by side; and then three
children, their faces terribly bloated and bluish,
still dressed in their tunics. They were silent then,
the real danger of their journey at last made plain
to them.

Suddenly Wulf remembered Oswald's warnings about the men of Deira and the need for
vengeance. He shook his head.

Only twelve monks at Lastingham had survived the plague. They quickly gathered and
eagerly welcomed the monks from Ythancestir.
Then Wulf and Brother Patrick immediately asked
about Cedd.

'He's alive,' said one monk. 'His own brothers
are with him now.'

'And your coming could help,' said another. 'If
anything could.'

How grave and how weary the Lastingham monks looked; Wulf shivered.

Then it was quickly arranged that the monks should go in twos and threes to the room where Cedd was lying, to present themselves and listen to whatever he might have to say to them, and this they began to do as soon as Cynebil, Cælin and Chad had left their brother's side . . .

Wulf did not enjoy waiting his turn as the monks went in order of seniority to see Cedd. Nor did he want to hear how the other monks found him. He wanted to find out for himself. He went alone to the monastery doors and sat outside them. The day's greyness had thinned again and there were sky-acres of blue. And somewhere nearby, an unseen cuckoo sung its melancholy two-tone song. Wulf sat there for an hour . . .

'Ah! You're here so,' said Brother Patrick, with the air of a man making a discovery.

Wulf started.

'Cedd wants to see you now. You're to see him alone.'

'Yes,' said Wulf. 'Yes.'

'That's what he wants.'

Wulf scrambled up and the two of them walked through the cool, gloomy monastery.

'You were always his special friend,' said Brother Patrick.

And then, on his own, his heart throbbing and throbbing, Wulf walked into the little room where Cedd was lying.

'Wulf,' said Cedd in a calm voice like that of a

man just after sleep and before sleep. 'Wulf, I knew thou'd come.'

Wulf dropped to his knees beside the pallet where Cedd lay, propped up on two bolsters. He didn't know whether to look or not to look at Cedd.

'I know,' said Cedd, stretching out his right hand and putting it on Wulf's head. 'I don't look much, I know. He's no beauty, thy Cedd.'

Then Wulf smiled at Cedd's customary bluntness, and was able to look at him, the black boils on his neck, the pallor of his skin, the terrible swelling of his glands that bloated his face.

'Oh! Wulf,' said Cedd. 'I ache now; I creak. I'll be glad to be rid of this body of mine.'

'No,' said Wulf quickly, dropping his head.

There was a moment's silence.

'Talk to me, or I'll sleep,' said Cedd. He moved his head slowly from side to side. 'Giddy,' he said. 'As if I were a child and you'd whirled me about.'

There were so many, many things Wulf had planned to say and wanted to say, but now he was actually with Cedd he was barely able to find words for his thoughts. 'You . . . I mean you . . . when you came to Ythancestir . . . ' Wulf began again. 'I was a child when you came to Ythancestir, and you whirled *me* about. You taught me about Christ. I became a Christian. You're, well, you know, you're sort of my father.'

'Aye,' said Cedd tenderly. 'I've given thee things and thou'st given me things. Aye, a sort of father; and thou'rt a sort of son,' Cedd smiled. 'And thou gavest me a place to build t'church.'

'That's true,' said Wulf.

'Aye!' said Cedd. 'On t'same spot where Wulf was christened on this day three years ago – t'first Christian among the East Saxons – I built t'church.'

'Three years today,' said Wulf wonderingly. 'And you remembered.'

Again they lapsed into silence.

'Wulf,' said Cedd, 'it's true, thou wert a boy then. And now thou'rt all but a man. Don't be afraid of this dying.'

Wulf felt choked in his throat. 'You may not,' he said.

'Remember all I've taught thee,' said Cedd firmly. 'And what if I do die?'

Wulf shook his head, his eyes flooded with tears.

'I'm not ashamed of this life of mine,' said Cedd. 'And I don't fear to die: God is gracious.'

'I've leaned on you and learned with you,' said Wulf.

'It's always so,' said Cedd. 'Fair enough to die, foul enough to live after the death of a loved one.'

Wulf bit his lower lip.

'Thou must labour profitably,' Cedd said. 'Grammar and psalms are they corner-stones . . . Restrain thy mind and hand and tongue and all t'other members of thy body . . . Never forget thy aims: help thy neighbour, as once thou helped thy brother Oswald; give food to t'hungry, drink to t'thirsty, and clothing to t'cold; take the poor wanderer into the monastery . . . Tell t'truth about Christ to one and all.'

Wulf nodded. He had heard Cedd say all the same things before; they sounded different now.

'In time to come,' said Cedd, 'thou'lt be a leader of men.'

Wulf frowned.

'Aye,' said Cedd. 'An Abbot and Bishop as I am. And thou'lt be a fine shaper of stone and bone, as fine as any East Saxon.' Cedd paused. He put his hands to his swollen face. 'I know these things, Wulf. In my bones I know them. God gives all men different gifts. Use thy great talents well.'

'Cedd,' said Wulf.

'My soul longs to see Christ,' said Cedd simply.

'Don't . . . ' said Wulf.

'Without me is not so different from with me. A man dies, he's buried in t'earth, but t'things he said, the way he taught, his strengths and weaknesses are remembered.' Cedd raised both hands, and joined them. 'I'll not die in thee, Wulf,' he said. 'I'll be thy earth-father.' He smiled weakly and Wulf found himself smiling back at him through his tears.

'I'll sing psalms with my brothers now,' said Cedd. 'Commend me to our brothers at Ythancestir. Tell them to work for Christ. Pray for me always, Wulf. And I, thy earth-father, shall intercede for thee with thy Father in heaven.'

Wulf left Cedd then. The mournful cuckoo was still singing nearby. Ewes with baby lambs at their heels were straying over the valley. Early April, almost night. In the blue hour, the colours around Wulf dimmed, the defined shapes of hill and tree and building all began to blur.

3

That night Cedd died. In his sleep, while his brother Chad knelt beside him, Cedd half-smiled, and took a deep breath and sighed.

Wulf saw that smile of peace, and gave thanks for it, when he knelt and prayed in Cedd's room the following morning. And though Cedd's face was blotched by the plague boils, and very grey, Wulf thought death had given it back its beauty. He looked around the room, at the weeping candles, the wooden cross in one corner, the comforting rough walls. He heard the heavy breathing of the monks. Then Wulf looked at Cedd again and it seemed to him that he was just asleep, and that if he touched him Cedd would wake.

Wulf thought of the things he had wanted to say to Cedd – how his life had been completely changed by Cedd's arrival in Ythancestir; how he had come to love him more than his own mother or brother or sister. His heart was almost bursting with the chances he thought he had missed and the pain of loss. He thought of those times together: Cedd's first coming in a boat dancing over the breakers; Cedd so calm when Oswald fired the monastery and all the other monks were panic-stricken; the day when Cedd had given him the Saulus spoon, promising to return in the spring.

And now he was gone in the spring . . . Wulf felt crushed by the company of monks and the weight of their sorrow. Quietly he left the room, and the monastery itself.

The cup of land in which the monastery had been built abounded with April life. The people in the tiny hamlet who had survived the plague were working under the sun. Cow and calf, sheep and lamb, uprooted and nibbled at greenest grass; and as much as they took, there was always more, every blade of grass was growing, pushing up and out of the earth, towards the sun. The trees were a blur of softest green, and the gorse was dazzling yellow, each bloom protected by stubborn prickles.

Wulf wandered alone. His chest was so constrained he felt as if it were bound with iron hoops like a bucket. He hugged his hurt to himself; his feelings about Cedd seemed far too precious to be shared. And then for the first time he thought he understood how Oswald could still nurse a terrible hurt and grudge at the death of their father, and resent Wulf travelling north to Deira.

The rocky high hills with their peat bogs and scrubby heather suited Wulf's mood better. He strayed further from Lastingham. The salt wind – sweeping in from the sea – bit into him.

But even as he walked, Wulf knew that he was not doing as Cedd would have wished, and thinking only for himself. After that first day, he stayed with the other monks, who were talking of building a new church in memory of Cedd, and even of staying for the remainder of their lives in Lastingham, near to his body; Wulf wondered if he would ever see Ythancestir again.

Shortly after Cedd's burial quite close to the monastery the plague reached out more black fingers. Brother Anselm the steersman . . . Brother Oswiu the lyre-player . . . Old Brother Edward the carver . . . in one day three of the brothers from Ythancestir were carried to the infirmary. One by one those who had resolved to build a church for Cedd, to house his body, entertained in their own bodies most unwelcome guests: dark spots under their arms; mushy swellings all over their bodies; shooting pains in their glands. Those who had debated whether or not to return to Ythancestir were spared the choice. Wulf knew he was unlikely to escape the plague. He watched and prayed and waited. Whenever he sniffed or sneezed, he thought it was a symptom; and all one day he lay wrapped in his mantle, shivering – certain his time had come.

Wulf found it hard to believe in God's mercy when he heard the groans of the monks. As one followed another to the infirmary, his mind was filled with gloom like a dark mist that would not rise. He started to think more and more about the time before he had met Cedd, the hours in the old fort when he told secrets about his dead father to the listening stones. 'If only . . . ' Wulf kept saying to himself. 'If only . . . ' But he was unable to complete the sentence.

One day Cedd's brother, Chad, said, 'You're not alone, Wulf. He was our brother. Your loss is our loss.'

The mist began to lift after that. Wulf felt released from himself; he talked and wept. He found himself looking forward as well as remembering.

But then the dark plague took Cynebil, Cedd's own brother, into its ghastly embrace. And after that it claimed Brother Patrick, whom Wulf loved next after Cedd himself, the man who had so often filled the air with gay laughter, and taught Wulf so much.

Those were black days; one by one every single monk who had come from Ythancestir with Wulf succumbed to a great heaviness, and felt the strength go out of his limbs.

Under sunlight, and sweeping bruised clouds, and outbursts of violent rain, sometimes all three at the same time, Wulf and Chad and Cælin and the only four survivors of the community at Lastingham buried the dead. They sang masses for them and said prayers for them.

At last one full week passed since any monk had been stricken with the plague . . . two weeks . . . three weeks . . . May grew near; the weather began to settle. And, as it did so, it became clear to the small group of men, and Wulf alone from Ythancestir, that they had indeed survived. They were not going to catch the plague. They walked about, they looked at the wonders of the world about them – the growing animals and plants, the enduring hills – and it all seemed new, almost as if they had never seen it before.

Then the seven survivors left Lastingham. Cælin went ahead, to take the news to Whitby and assure Abbess Hild there was no risk now that they could be carriers of the plague.

Wulf and Chad and the four monks from Lastingham followed three days after; and Wulf carried with him the manuscript Brother Patrick had borrowed from the library at Ythancestir, and a small stave of wood on which Brother Edward had already carved a sinewy wolf with a long scroll of a tail. When they reached Whitby, Abbess Hild welcomed them, and Finan the Bishop was there from Lindisfarne to greet them. Wulf looked about him and saw men laughing and talking as well as tender, and thought he was dreaming and could not wake.

Finan took Wulf aside into the cloister, and soon asked him, 'Will you go back to Ythancestir?'

'Of course!' said Wulf. The way south was the way back to his place, the monastery, and the way back to his family – he kept thinking of Anna running to meet him from the hut, as she always did, her fair hair streaming behind her.

'The wind's right,' said Finan.

'On my own?' asked Wulf.

'I've brought thirty monks here from Hexham and Jarrow and Lindisfarne,' said the Bishop. 'Will you take them and guide them?'

Wulf looked up at the old bishop eagerly. 'Thirty monks!'

'I sent one south yesterday to say you're coming. Brother Wilfred will be expecting you.'

Wulf shivered. He was suddenly filled with an overwhelming desire to have the wind in his sails, and to be on his way once more.

'Cedd told me about you,' said Finan.

'Did he?' said Wulf, surprised and pleased.

'You'll continue his work, as he taught you?'

'I will,' said Wulf.

'We need you,' said Finan. 'The work is only just beginning. The great tree is growing: it puts down roots, and rises and wins leaves and loses them, always stronger each spring.'

Wulf knitted his brows, and slowly nodded.

'Don't be too proud to share your sorrows just as you share your joys,' said Finan, looking shrewdly at Wulf. Then he put his hand on Wulf's head. 'Go tomorrow. Take Cedd alive in you.'

'I will,' said Wulf.

'So, the green blade rises from the buried corn,' said Finan.

Day dawned. The lightening of the sky in the east, palish green and grey, woke Wulf. Or perhaps it was the birds that woke him, one and another and another and a whole congregation carolling over the return of the light. Wulf leaped up, instantly awake, as if he never had been tired; everything seemed possible.

Another monk was awake somewhere, for soon the bell for Matins began to toll. And after all the monks had praised God and prayed for His grace, and eaten in the refectory, the travellers were eager to be away. Wulf led thirty men down to the water's edge, and there they made their farewells and embarked.

The boat cut a silver swathe through the dark waves, a strong line away south. To the east the horizon was still blurred, and to the west lay undulating land. The sea-fret stung them; it tasted good.

One monk, quite young, asked Wulf, 'What's it like?'

And another, 'How long will we be?'

And a third, 'What was he like, Wulf?'

Wulf closed his eyes and opened his eyes. He could see a boat, bucking and rocking, closing with a stone jetty. The jetty was packed with people: some were smiling, some crying; and they were all waving.